Seal Child

For Anna, thank-you! ~ R V

For my mother and father who, with courage and hope, found a safe new home for generations to come. ~ A P

American edition published in 2021
by New Frontier Publishing Europe Ltd
www.newfrontierpublishing.us

First published in the UK in 2021
by New Frontier Publishing Europe Ltd
Uncommon, 126 New King's Road, London SW6 4LZ, United Kingdom
www.newfrontierpublishing.co.uk

ISBN: 978-1-913639-40-2

Distributed in the United States and Canada by Lerner Publishing Group Inc.
241 First Avenue North, Minneapolis, MN 55401 USA
www.lernerbooks.com

Library of Congress Cataloging-in-Publication data is available.

Designed by Verity Clark

Printed in China
10 9 8 7 6 5 4 3 2 1

Seal Child

Robert Vescio   Anna Pignataro

NEW FRONTIER PUBLISHING

Once, life was peaceful.

Until . . .

... the storm hit.

And then it was just me.

Under a darkened sky,
I waited for a sign.

I called out.

But no answer came.

I ran down to the water
and saw a baby seal,
alone on the beach.

Its mother must have been
too afraid to return.

I found an abandoned boat.

I carried the pup and
pushed the boat out
to sea.

I hurried to get away,
afraid the storm
would follow us.

The water went on forever.

Tears clouded my eyes, as the sadness crept in.

I felt far.

I felt lost.

I stroked the pup. Its whiskers quivered.
Its body shivered.

Then it stared into my eyes and yelped.
The pup made me smile. And I felt better.

For many days and nights,

I searched for a place
the storm hadn't hit.

I was scared of the monsters lurking beneath my boat.

So I would tell happy stories to the pup.

I floated through weather that was kind . . .

. . . and weather that was cruel.

The nights were especially cold.

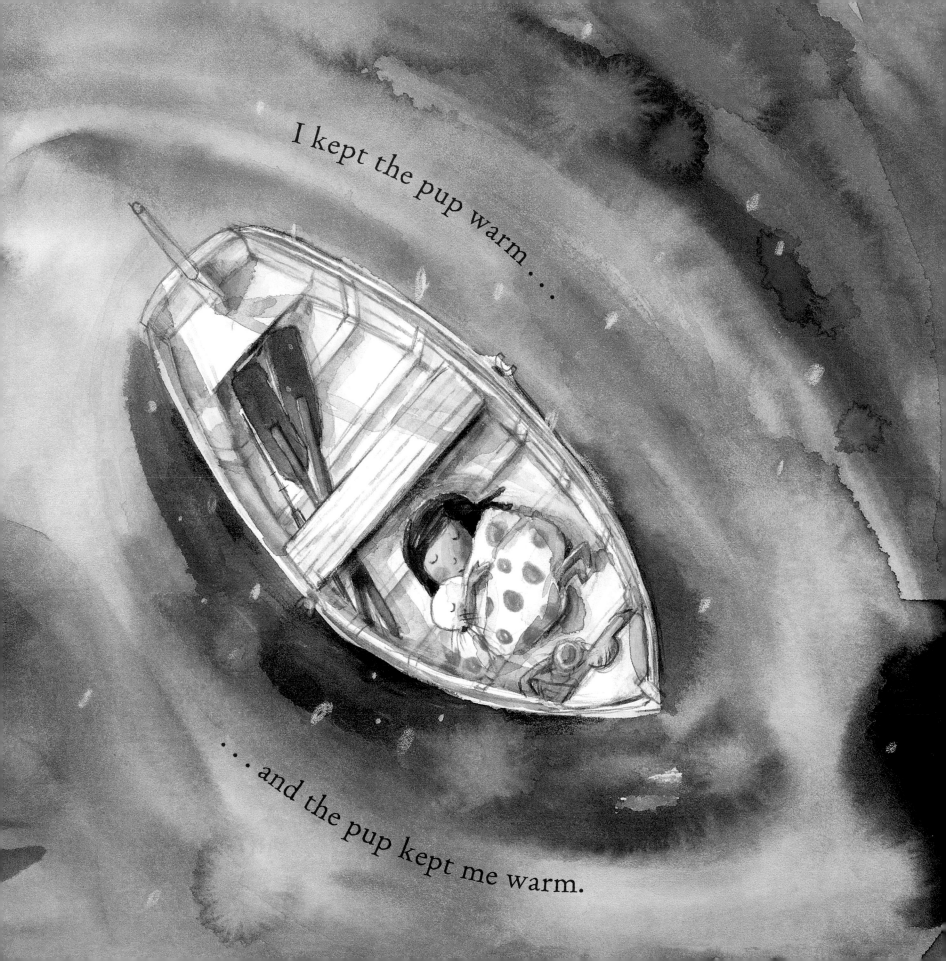

I kept the pup warm . . .

. . . and the pup kept me warm.

I taught the pup how to swim.
The pup always remained close,
splashing and riding in the waves.

Until one day . . .

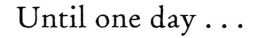

. . . I was surrounded
by sound.

There was movement
underneath me.

I was scared it
was a **monster,**
ready to **gobble**
me up.

Another seal appeared. It came nose
to nose with the pup.

The pup cried with joy as it snuggled
up against its mother.

At last . . .

... a **sweet** surprise.

When I reached the shore, I turned and saw
the flash of a flipper, waving in the water.

Then, with a playful leap, the pup spun in the air and plunged into the water, making a huge splash.

I should have been pleased
but I felt sad.

I was just as lost as before.
I missed the pup.

It felt strange to be alone.
There was no one to listen.

But then my eyes cleared.

Something appeared in the distance.

It washed the sadness away.

It drove the ache out of my heart . . .

. . . and I felt **safe** again.